EVIL DECEPTICON

Megatron, leader of the Decepticons, is ruthless and cunning. He transforms from a gun to lead the Decepticons in their fight against the Autobots.

Soundwave transforms from a cassette recorder to a Decepticon communicator robot and acts as a radio link for the other Decepticons. He is able to read minds and will use blackmail for his own gain. Soundwave is despised by all other Decepticons.

Laserbeak is cowardly and will run for safety if he is threatened. He can fly at speeds of up to 250 mph and transforms from a spy cassette to the Decepticon interrogation robot.

Starscream transforms from a plane to the Decepticon air commander robot. He can fly faster than any of the Decepticons and seeks to replace Megatron as leader. Starscream is ruthless and cruel.

Rumble is small and tough. When he transforms from a spy cassette to the demolition robot, he transmits low frequency groundwaves to create powerful earthquakes.

Ravage likes to operate alone and is the craftiest of all Decepticons. He transforms from a spy cassette to a saboteur robot. He is very good at hiding himself in the shadows of the night and can walk without making a sound.

The heroic warriors, the Autobots, and their enemies, the evil Decepticons, have landed on Earth from their own planet, Cybertron.

The battle between the forces of good and evil continues on Earth as the Transformers change to robots and back again, in an attempt to outwit or deceive each other in their struggle for power.

British Library Cataloguing in Publication Data

Grant, John, 1930-
    Autobots' lightning strike.—(Transformers, Series 853; v. 1)
    I. Title II. Farmer, Mark III. Collins, Mike IV. Series
    823'.914[J]   PZ7
    ISBN 0-7214-0895-8

First edition

THE TRANS™ FORMERS

AUTOBOTS' LIGHTNING STRIKE

written by JOHN GRANT
illustrated by MIKE COLLINS and MARK FARMER

Ladybird Books Loughborough

Spike, the young engineer and friend of the Autobots, sat on a rock in the warm sunshine writing up his diary. The air was fresh after the storm which had raged during the night. The rain had fallen in torrents. The thunder had boomed and crashed. And the lightning had lit the innermost parts of the Autobot base.

"It was strange," wrote Spike. "The Autobots thought that they were being attacked by the Decepticons. They rushed to action stations. Optimus Prime and Jazz were ready to repel an attack, when the storm passed on. It seems that thunder and lightning are unknown on their planet of Cybertron. It must be a very strange world."

Spike put the diary in his pocket and made his way back to the base.

As he drew near, a giant, gleaming figure came towards him. It was Optimus Prime, the Autobot Leader. He looked down at Spike. "This is a very strange world, this Earth of yours," he said.

Spike grinned. "Funny," he said. "I was just thinking something like that myself."

Other Autobots came out into the open. Hound pointed to a steep rock face some distance away. "Look at that mountain! It didn't look like that yesterday!"

"Half of it's gone," cried Jazz.

"It must have been struck by lightning," said Spike.

"You mean those bright lights?" said Sunstreaker.

"Whatever it was, it must have been powerful," replied Sideswipe.

Spike's father joined them. "Lightning is dangerous stuff," he said. "I've seen it wreck buildings, fell trees, sink oil rigs. Even a small bolt of lightning can pack a hefty punch."

Optimus Prime looked thoughtful. The Autobots were desperate to find a source of energy so that they could rebuild their spacecraft and return to Cybertron. Could the answer lie in this thing called lightning?

"Tell me all you know about lightning," said Optimus Prime.

Spike's father picked up a piece of twig and drew diagrams in the earth as he spoke.

"Lightning is really electricity," he said.

"We have electricity on Cybertron," said Optimus Prime. "But it does not fall from the sky and destroy things. We generate it in power stations. It drives our machines."

"We also do that here on Earth," said Spike's father. "But there is no way to control something as powerful as lightning. A single lightning flash is about a thousand megavolts."

"Perhaps Earth technology cannot handle such forces," said Optimus Prime. "On Cybertron we learned to deal with power you cannot even begin to imagine. This is a chance we cannot afford to miss. The Autobots must be prepared before the next storm. Tell Huffer I must speak to him."

As usual, Huffer complained. "Lightning!" he muttered. "Catch it! You want it put in a cage, I suppose?"

"If you think that's best, then do it by all means," said Optimus Prime. "Just as long as it's ready before the next thunderstorm."

For the next week Huffer was hardly to be seen. He transformed into his truck disguise and went off on lone searches for materials. Once he returned to base to borrow some tools from Ratchet. "Lightning! Energy convertors!" he complained to Ratchet. "None of this nonsense on Cybertron! If I was back there now...!"

Another time, Huffer asked Gears to help him to lift some heavy components. Although Gears complained, he did help but each of them pretended to be more miserable than the other.

Huffer worked hard on the project and finally it was finished. He rolled in one day and spoke to Optimus Prime. "I suppose you'll want to see it," he said. "Don't suppose I'll get any thanks – just a worn clutch and a slow puncture."

Huffer escorted his Leader to a distant mountain. He pointed ahead. Optimus Prime could see nothing unusual. "Where is it?" he asked.

Huffer activated a control on his chest plate, and from the top of the mountain, there rose a slender lattice of gleaming metal. Slowly, it rose up and stood with its top partly hidden by drifting clouds.

"According to the Earth people, lightning most often strikes tall objects," said Huffer. "There is your lightning collector – it's the tallest thing for hundreds of kilometres."

"How do we extract the power from the lightning?" asked Optimus Prime.

"Under the mountain," said Huffer, "is a cavern. There I have built the energy convertor. We will have a test run during the next thunderstorm."

"Let's hope that the Decepticons do not find out," said Optimus Prime.

But as he spoke, a winged messenger was already on its way back to Decepticon headquarters. It was Laserbeak, carrying news of the latest Autobot activity back to Megatron, Leader of the Decepticons.

Megatron studied Laserbeak's report. He sent for Soundwave. "What does it sound like to you?" he asked.

"It must be a radio mast of some sort," said Soundwave. "From its size and location it must have great range, both for sending and receiving."

"Who are the Autobots sending messages to?"
asked Starscream, angrily. "Perhaps there are
other Autobots we know nothing about. We must
destroy this thing before it is too late! Now!"

"*I* make the decisions," snapped Megatron.
"Soundwave, Laserbeak will lead you to the place.
Keep a listening watch. This creation of theirs
may be very useful to us."

"I still say that we should destroy it!" said
Starscream. "If I were Leader, the last Autobot
would have long since been reduced to a handful
of rusting nuts and bolts!"

Guided by Laserbeak, Soundwave went swiftly to the lonely mountain. He stood on a nearby hill. "Where is it?" he asked. "Where is the tall metal radio mast. I see nothing."

The top of the mountain was bare.

Laserbeak flew up and circled in the sky above the peak. There was nothing to be seen.

Soundwave was about to leave the hill-top when his audio-sensors caught a faint signal. It sounded like running machinery and it seemed to come from somewhere under the ground.

Laserbeak gave a sudden screech. There was movement on the mountain peak. Something rose slowly from among the rocks. As Soundwave watched, Huffer's lightning collector rose into the sky until its top was lost in the haze. Deep in the underground chamber, Huffer made some adjustments as he tested the machine, unaware that he was being spied upon.

For hours, Soundwave remained on the hill-top. He tuned his audio-sensors to their finest pitch. He tried every frequency but there was not a whisper of a radio signal. There was nothing coming from the mast at all. No radio! No infra-red! No ultra-violet! Whatever system the Autobots had devised, it was quite undetectable, even to an expert like Soundwave.

Megatron must be told of this, without delay. Soundwave made all speed back to Decepticon headquarters.

"Destroy it, and the Autobots with it!" shrieked Starscream, when he heard Soundwave's news.

Megatron looked thoughtful. "This technology is beyond even *our* wildest dreams. If we can learn its secret we will have a powerful weapon. Laserbeak, you will return and keep watch on the Autobots while I make my plans."

Megatron did not notice Starscream whisper to Rumble and slip away from the rest of the group.

Not knowing that they were being watched, the Autobots made the final preparations for the first test of the lightning energy convertor. Powerful cables were led from the base of the mast, deep into the mountain and then connected to the equipment in the chamber.

Gears muttered to himself, and to anyone else who would listen, that the whole thing was ridiculous. "What if there isn't another storm?" he said. "What if there's no more lightning?"

"There *will* be a thunderstorm sooner or later," said Spike's father. "We have to wait."

"OK. We wait," said Gears. "We've only been on this Earth of yours for four million years. So, let's wait!"

"We can pick up weather reports from the radio," said Spike. "They'll tell us when a storm is due."

"Cheer up, Gears," said Bluestreak. "If there isn't a storm we can fly a flag on Huffer's mast!"

Laserbeak watched the Autobots from high in the sky. He flew close to the top of the metal mast. He perched on the swaying structure while his sensors recorded all its details.

As darkness fell, the bird-like robot spiralled down the height of the mast. He was watching the activity on the ground. And suddenly, he spotted something new.

There was an opening in the foot of the mountain. Autobots were coming out. So were the two Earth-men who had befriended them.

Laserbeak stayed perched on the struts of the mast. Unseen in the dusk, he watched the Autobots transform at Optimus Prime's command. Spike and his father climbed into Huffer's cab. Then, in a blaze of headlights, the Autobots swept in a long line round the foot of the mountain and back towards their base.

Laserbeak arrived at the Decepticon headquarters, transforming to his other disguise as an audio-cassette. Soundwave slotted the cassette into his playback system and the Decepticons listened to the description of all that Laserbeak had observed.

The steel mast was still a mystery. But now it appeared that the Autobots had made something which was hidden *inside* the mountain.

"I must know what is so important that they have buried it," said Megatron. "I cannot tolerate those creatures knowing something that I do not. We will tear their secret from them!" He called for Starscream but Frenzy said that he'd seen him go off with Rumble.

Megatron roared with rage. "The mindless vandal! I can guess what he's planning," he cried. "We must stop him immediately! Decepticons... SCRAMBLE!"

The entire Decepticon force rose into the air and raced at top speed to stop Starscream before he destroyed the Autobots and their secret.

Spike stood by the radio, trying to tune into a local station, to catch the weather forecast:

"The sky is clouding over," he said. "I shouldn't be surprised if there was another storm soon."

He turned the dial again and there were a few bars of music. The music stopped and a man's voice spoke:

"Here is the local weather outlook for the next twenty-four hours. Temperatures will stay the same, but a moist, warm airstream from the west will move in later, with a strong possibility of thunderstorms over the mountains."

"This is it!" cried Spike. "A storm coming up!"

"What a planet," muttered Gears. "There's going to be a storm...so that's good?"

"If Huffer's equipment is ready," said Optimus Prime, "let's not waste time. Autobots... TRANSFORM!"

In a moment the Autobots, with Spike and his father in Huffer's cab, were making their way to the mountain and the lightning energy convertor.

Storm clouds were already gathering as the Autobots reached the mountain. A few spots of rain fell.

"At least we'll be under cover in the chamber under the mountain," said Jazz.

"I wouldn't advise that," said Huffer. "We know nothing about this lightning thing. I intend to conduct this test from as far away as possible."

"There's an overhanging cliff over there," said Optimus Prime. "We'll be out of the storm but still able to see the mountain."

Taking up their positions, the Autobots watched as Huffer activated the control on his chest panel. Slowly, the slender mast of the lightning collector rose from the top of the mountain.

The clouds began to swirl around the lattice as the first rumbles of the storm sounded in the distance.

In the gathering gloom, no one noticed Starscream and Rumble as they slipped into the entrance to the underground chamber.

Starscream stopped in the centre of the
chamber and looked about him. The walls and
roof were bare rock. The floor was paved with
smooth plastic sheeting. And in the centre of the
floor rose a mighty piece of machinery.

Starscream walked all around it. From each
corner of a head-high stone base there rose a
smooth silver column. Each column supported a
silver sphere. Between the columns was a
complicated mass of insulators and cables.
Nothing moved. It was silent.

Rumble grew impatient. "I thought we were going to smash this," he said. "Two low frequency jolts and it'll be just another heap of junk!"

"It's not *doing* anything," said Starscream. "It doesn't work! And that run-down museum piece we have for a leader thought that it was a secret radio system!"

Starscream roared with laughter. But even as his laughter echoed around the rocky chamber, a voice rang out!

Megatron strode across the chamber, his fusion-cannon aimed steadily at Starscream. "Traitor!" he roared. "Saboteur! Against my orders, you would destroy this machine? And I am a run-down museum piece, am I?"

"I sought only to serve you and the Decepticon cause," said Starscream, grovelling before Megatron. "The Autobots want to destroy us. This fiendish device will harm us."

"But it does nothing! You said so yourself," cried Megatron. "They have extended their aerial. We saw that as we arrived. No doubt at this very moment they are preparing to send or receive a signal. If they have friends, or if there are other Autobots on this planet, I want to know. Then we shall crush them all!"

From the shelter of the cliff, the Autobots peered up at the mast as the storm passed overhead.

Lightning flashed among the storm clouds. It glared blue and white among the dark clouds. The light made bright reflections on the metal lattice of Huffer's mast.

"Very pretty, I'm sure," said Jazz. "When is it going to do something useful – like making that contraption work inside the mountain?"

"Contraption?" cried Huffer. "If your head had more in it than loose nuts and bolts you wouldn't say things like that. My lightning energy convertor is *not* a contraption. Just be patient!"

"Wait! Be patient! You sound more like an Earth-man every day," said Gears. "If I didn't... WOW! What was that?"

With an earsplitting crash, a jagged fork of lightning crackled out of the clouds and hit the tip of the mast. It was followed by another! And another!

In a swift ripple of blue fire the lightning ran down the mast and into the mountain!

Inside the mountain, Rumble was trying to hide himself, away from Megatron's fury, when a great surge of power knocked the Decepticons flying in all directions.

There was a roaring in the air. Metal bodies clanged and clattered as they fell. And from the machine in the centre of the chamber there was a splutter and crackle as the energy convertor took the lightning charge.

The chamber was now lit by the blue and white light from the machine. The electricity arced and crackled and the silver spheres glowed with power.

Slowly the Decepticons struggled to their feet.

"It does nothing? It doesn't work?" roared Megatron. Starscream cringed silently in the shadows. "What are they saying? What message are they transmitting?" Megatron shouted to Soundwave above the noise.

Soundwave adjusted his controls. "I can't tell," he said. "Something has happened to my audio-radio sensor. It's malfunctioning. I get nothing but static."

As he spoke there was a loud hiss and a crack. A long blue arc of electricity shot from the machine and struck the rocky roof of the chamber.

The electricity ran across the roof, then down the walls. They glowed and flickered with the blue light. Skywarp put out a hand to touch one wall. Next moment he had been hurled in a shower of sparks across the chamber.

Skywarp lay on the floor, still giving off sparks. He tried to rise, but instead he began to transform. The transformation stopped halfway. Then with another shower of sparks he returned to his plane disguise. "Major malfunction to report," he said.

But the others weren't listening. Their eyes were on Starscream. "If this machine can be started, then it can also be stopped," he shouted.

He aimed the null-ray projector at one of the silver spheres and fired. As the ray hit the sphere the electricity ran back down it to Starscream. He was sent sprawling across the floor. The null-ray projector was scorched and buckled. It was useless.

"It's an Autobot trap!" cried Megatron. "RETREAT!"

Megatron led the way to the chamber entrance.
The air now seemed alive with electrical energy.
It arced and sparked from the walls and onto the
metal bodies of the Decepticons. Control systems
and sensors malfunctioned. Wiring began to burn
out. Fuses blew.

A cassette shot from Soundwave's chest pack
and transformed into Ravage. The mechanical
hound, with all his systems malfunctioning, gave a
snarl. Then it hurled itself in a savage attack on
Megatron – its own Leader.

Megatron hit out with his metal fist and Ravage
was thrown to the floor in a shower of sparks.
Soundwave grabbed the creature and dragged it
towards the entrance.

But the electricity had been too quick for the
stumbling Decepticons. As they reached the
rocky arch which led to the open air, the
flickering light shot across the opening, forming a
curtain of electrical energy.

As the retreating Decepticons battled through,
creaking and spluttering, they were spotted by the
Autobots. Through the rain which was now
pouring down, the Autobots looked in amazement
at their scorched and battered enemies.

"Where did *they* come from?" said Optimus
Prime.

Hound watched the Decepticons as they made their way into the open. The rain hissed on hot metal. After they had gone, a train of smoke hung in the air.

"I thought that I had picked up their signals when they first arrived," said Hound, "but I wasn't sure. It seems that they thought our energy collector was a radio transmitter. They were trying to discover its secrets."

"Well, they certainly got the message!" said Jazz.

Huffer pressed the controls on his chest plate. The mast disappeared into the mountain. Then he went inside to inspect the energy convertor.

"It's a bit bent in places," he said when he rejoined the others. "And I haven't got it quite right. It needs some more work on it."

As they prepared to leave, Optimus Prime looked across at the mountain. The storm had passed and the moon shone in a clear sky.

"Energy from the sky will help us to return to our own world," he said. "It will also be our gift to the people of Earth after we have gone."

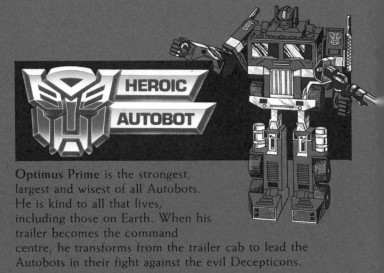

Optimus Prime is the strongest,
largest and wisest of all Autobots.
He is kind to all that lives,
including those on Earth. When his
trailer becomes the command
centre, he transforms from the trailer cab to lead the
Autobots in their fight against the evil Decepticons.

Hound transforms from a four-wheel-drive vehicle to the
Autobot scout robot. He is brave and loyal to the Autobot
cause and likes the planet Earth. Secretly, Hound would like
to be human!

Sideswipe transforms from a racing car to a warrior robot.
He and his twin brother, Sunstreaker, make a powerful
team in the never-ending battle against the Decepticons.

Huffer transforms from a trailer cab to become the Autobot
construction engineer. Although he will mutter and
complain, he is a strong and reliable worker.

Jazz transforms from a racing car to the Autobot special
operations agent. He takes on the dangerous missions and is
clever and daring. He likes Earth and is always looking to
learn more about the planet and its people.

Gears transforms from an armoured carrier to work as a
transport and reconnaissance robot. Like Huffer, he likes to
be miserable and find fault in everything, but he has great
strength and endurance.